GRANDPA GAZiLLiON'S NUMBER YARD

BY

Laurie Keller

HENRY HOLT ᵃⁿᵈ COMPANY

New York

SQUARE FISH

SQUARE
FISH

An Imprint of Macmillan
175 Fifth Avenue
New York, NY 10010
mackids.com

Our books may be purchased in bulk for promotional, educational, or business use. Please contact
your local bookseller or the Macmillan Corporate and Premium Sales Department at (800) 221-7945 ext. 5442
or by e-mail at MacmillanSpecialMarkets@macmillan.com.

Library of Congress Cataloging-in-Publication Data
Keller, Laurie. Grandpa Gazillion's number yard / by Laurie Keller.
p.   cm.
Summary: Grandpa Gazillion and Hildegarde show many different uses
for the numbers one through twenty at their number yard.
ISBN 978-1-250-09537-4 (paperback)
[1. Counting. 2. Stories in rhyme.] I. Title.
PZ8.3.K294Gr 2005   [E]–dc22   2004023394

Originally published in the United States by Henry Holt and Company, LLC
First Square Fish Edition: 2016
Book designed by Donna Mark
Square Fish logo designed by Filomena Tuosto
The artist used acrylic paint on Arches watercolor
paper to create the illustrations for this book.

1 3 5 7 9 10 8 6 4 2

AR: 3.2 / LEXILE: AD650L

need a
NUMBER?
Grandpa
G's
ot it!

nice
try
pal.

I'm Grandpa Gazillion, and she's Hildegarde.
Welcome, dear friends, to my ol' number yard.

Numbers aren't used just for counting these days.
Old numbers help people in many new ways.

Take Elmo Alfonzo McFizzleby's wife—
Last year on vacation a FOUR saved her life!

So go fetch some numbers (oh, twenty will do),
And let's see how numbers can help you out, too!

LOOK OUT—a volcano of hot mac 'n' cheese!
Don't worry, a **ONE** makes a nifty trapeze.

No music or dancing up there on the moon?
Get the place jumpin'—play a catchy TWO tune.

3 If your double-humped camel annoys your backside,
Saddle up with a THREE for a smooth, easy ride.

You're soaked head to toe from the elephant's splash.
Go plug in a FOUR—you'll be dry in a flash.

You're buried beneath mashed potatoes and chives?
A **FIVE** snorkel lets you breathe till help arrives.

Don't you hate when your eyebrows fall into your soup?
Dig them out with a SIX—it's a great eyebrow scoop!

Oh, YUCK! Spinach ice cream tastes just like cow dung!
A SEVEN scrapes bad tastes right off of your tongue.

8

Do your gym socks fall down when you run really fast?
An **EIGHT** holds them up (but you might finish last).

You're hungry and stuck on a tall mountain peak?
A lollipop NINE can last up to a week!

You can't see the parade 'cause the crowd is too thick?
Get a great view on your **TEN** pogo stick.

A skunk had some "perfume" she wanted to share.
Stand on an ELEVEN and get some fresh air.

If the snores from next door are disturbing your sleep,
Plug your ears with a TWELVE and you won't hear a peep.

OH NO—your plaid parachute's full of plaid holes!
A **THIRTEEN** will save you (watch out for flagpoles).

Your pink plastic pig is refusing to float?
Get back to dry land on a **FOURTEEN** sailboat.

You're covered with germs (you stood next to some sneezers).
A **FIFTEEN** removes them—it works just like tweezers.

16

You've just been sat on by a giant meatball!
Pick up your **SIXTEEN** phone and give him a call.

The toads are upset—someone broke their toadstools!
Fix them in a snap with your **SEVENTEEN** tools.

18

Your neighbor's long mustache keeps tickling your face?
An **EIGHTEEN** hairclip holds it neatly in place.

If the birds down the street ask you over to dine,
Put on a **NINETEEN** and you'll fit in just fine.

Special delivery—a big, hairy gift.
A **TWENTY** pushcart makes him easy to lift.

See, what did I tell you—aren't numbers the best?
They always come through when they're put to the test.

If you're in a pickle, a bind, or a fix,
Just try out a FIFTEEN, a TEN, or a SIX.

Finding new uses for numbers is fun.
You've got a big brain, you could think of a ton.

So wherever you go and whatever you do
Take my advice—keep your numbers with you!